4

D1540639

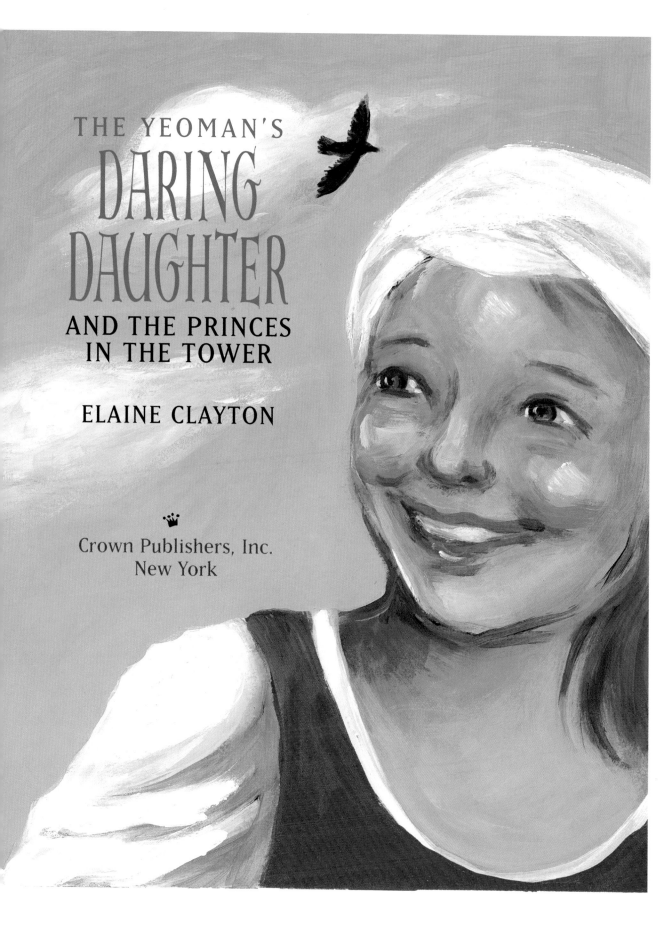

THE YEOMAN'S DARING DAUGHTER

AND THE PRINCES IN THE TOWER

ELAINE CLAYTON

Crown Publishers, Inc.
New York

Interior hand lettering by Bernard Maisner

Published by Crown Publishers, Inc., a Random House company, 201 East 50th Street, New York, NY 10022
CROWN is a trademark of Crown Publishers, Inc.

Library of Congress Cataloging-in-Publication Data
Clayton, Elaine.
The yeoman's daring daughter and the princes in the tower / Elaine Clayton. — 1st ed.
p. cm.
Summary: In 1483, the daughter of a guard at the royal palace exchanges notes with the two young princes
who have been locked in the Tower of London by their uncle Richard, so he can become king.
1. Edward IV, King of England, 1470-1483—Juvenile fiction. 2. Richard, Duke of York, 1473-1483—Juvenile fiction. [1. Edward IV,
King of England, 1470-1483—Fiction. 2. Richard, Duke of York, 1473-1483—Fiction. 3. Great Britain—History—Richard III,
1483-1485—Fiction. 4. Letters—Fiction.] I. Title.
PZ7.C57917Ye   1999
[E]—dc21   98-20573

ISBN   0-517-70984-8 (trade)   0-517-70985-6 (lib. bdg.)
Printed in Singapore   www.randomhouse.com/kids   10 9 8 7 6 5 4 3 2 1   First Edition

For Jonah Barry

with thanks to
Tracy and Isabel

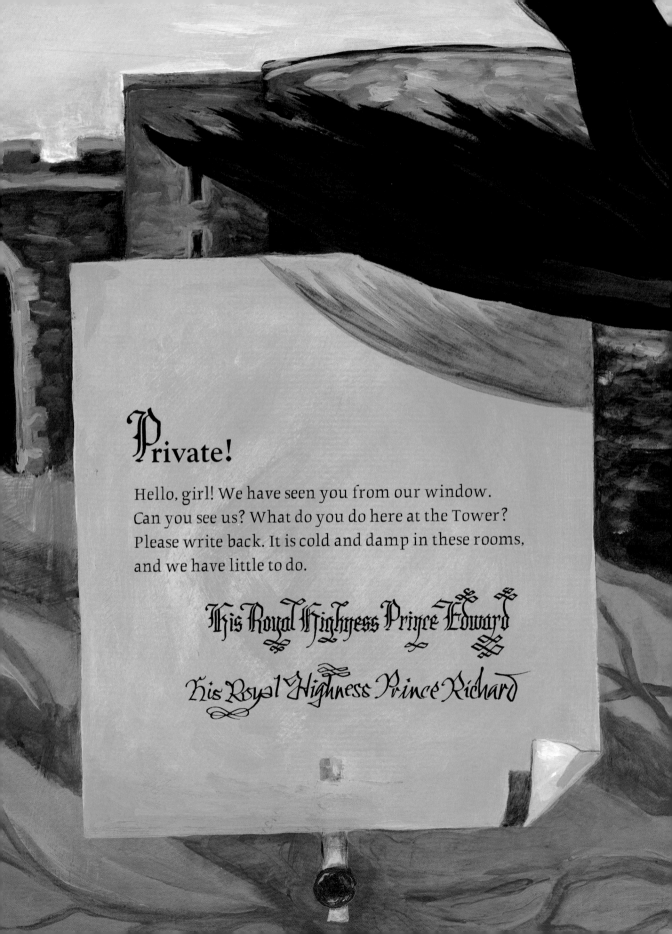

Private!

Hello, girl! We have seen you from our window.
Can you see us? What do you do here at the Tower?
Please write back. It is cold and damp in these rooms,
and we have little to do.

His Royal Highness Prince Edward

His Royal Highness Prince Richard

Private!

Dear Prince Edward and Prince Richard,
I am a Yeoman's daughter. My father guards this
royal fortress. I have many duties here at the Tower—
I help with the cleaning and the mending. My raven,
Jewel, carried this message to you. If you are really
the princes, why aren't you at the palace?

Jane, daughter of a Yeoman of the Crown·

Private!

Dear Jane,

When our father, King Edward IV, died, our uncle, Richard, Duke of Gloucester, brought us to the Tower. He said we would be safe here until Coronation Day. I, Edward, shall be the next King! Richard, my younger brother, will have to wait his turn—he is heir apparent. Perhaps you can come to the coronation!

His Royal Highness Prince Edward

His Royal Highness Prince Richard

Private!

Dear Prince Edward and Prince Richard,
I have a surprise for you! The Keeper of the
Royal Wardrobe has asked me to help sew
your vestments for your coronation!

Jane

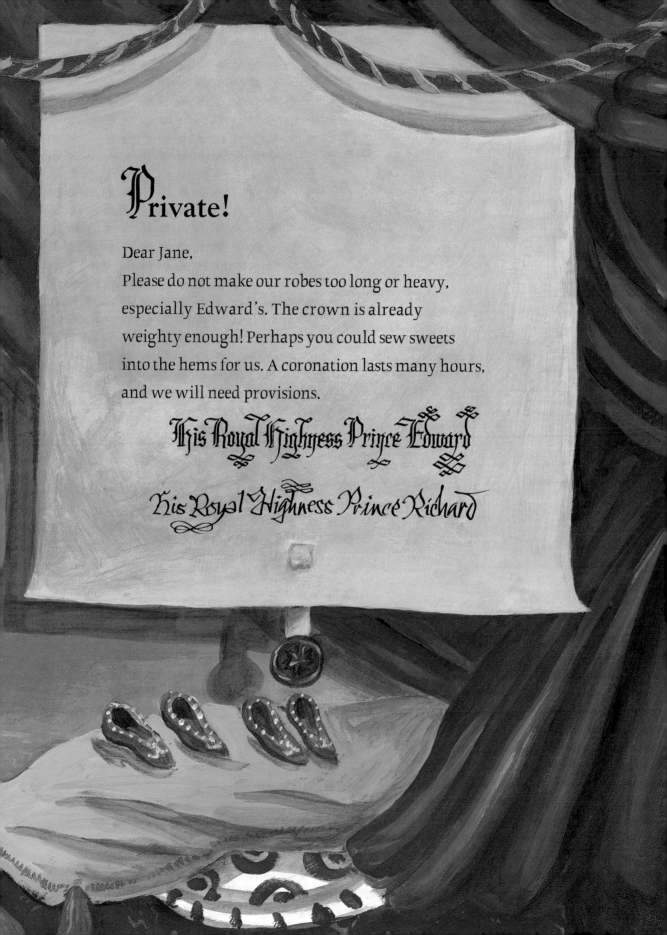

Private!

Dear Jane,

Please do not make our robes too long or heavy,
especially Edward's. The crown is already
weighty enough! Perhaps you could sew sweets
into the hems for us. A coronation lasts many hours,
and we will need provisions.

His Royal Highness Prince Edward

His Royal Highness Prince Richard

Private!

Dear Prince Edward and Prince Richard,
Today, I overheard a very wicked plan.
I fear that your uncle may not be trusted.
Please be careful!

Jane

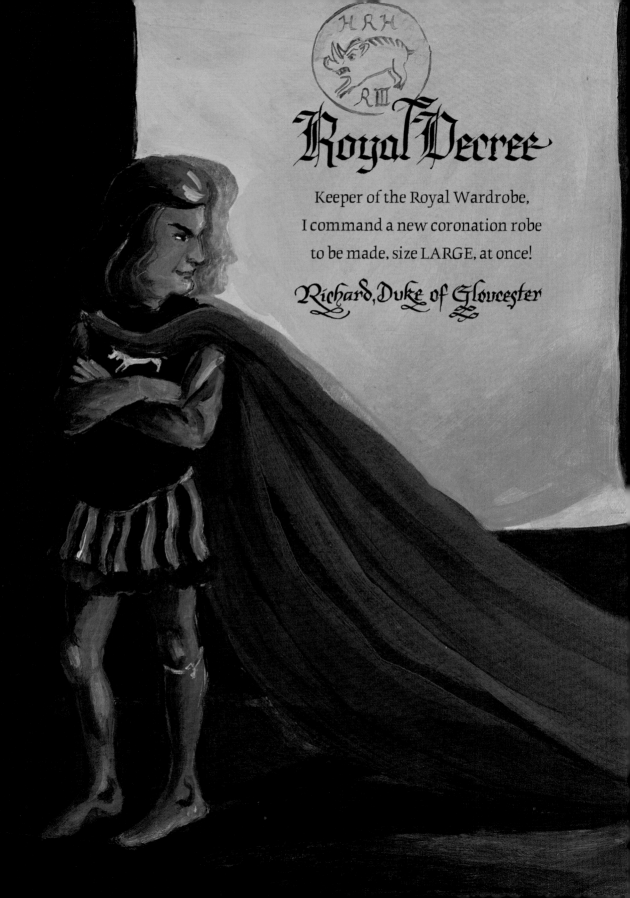

Royal Decree

Keeper of the Royal Wardrobe,
I command a new coronation robe
to be made, size LARGE, at once!

Richard, Duke of Gloucester

Private!

Dear Prince Edward and Prince Richard,
Your lives are in danger! I have found
the key to your chambers. At dusk,
I will come for you.
Speak of this to no one!

You know who

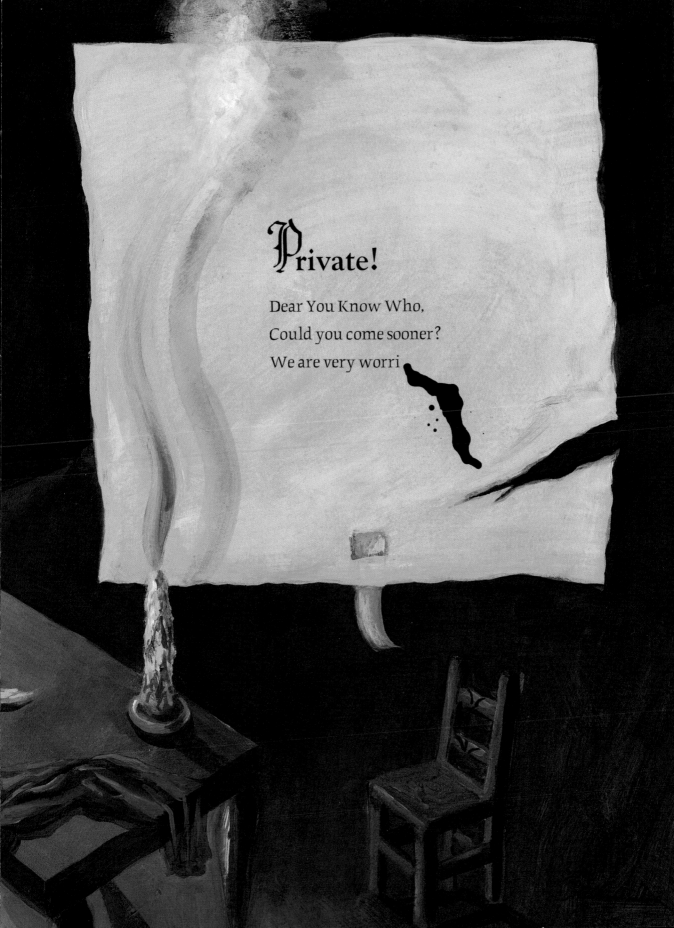

Royal Decree

Constable and Yeomen of the Crown,
I have discovered the princes missing from their chambers.
Whosoever finds and delivers them to me shall be richly rewarded.
Make haste!

Richard, Duke of Gloucester

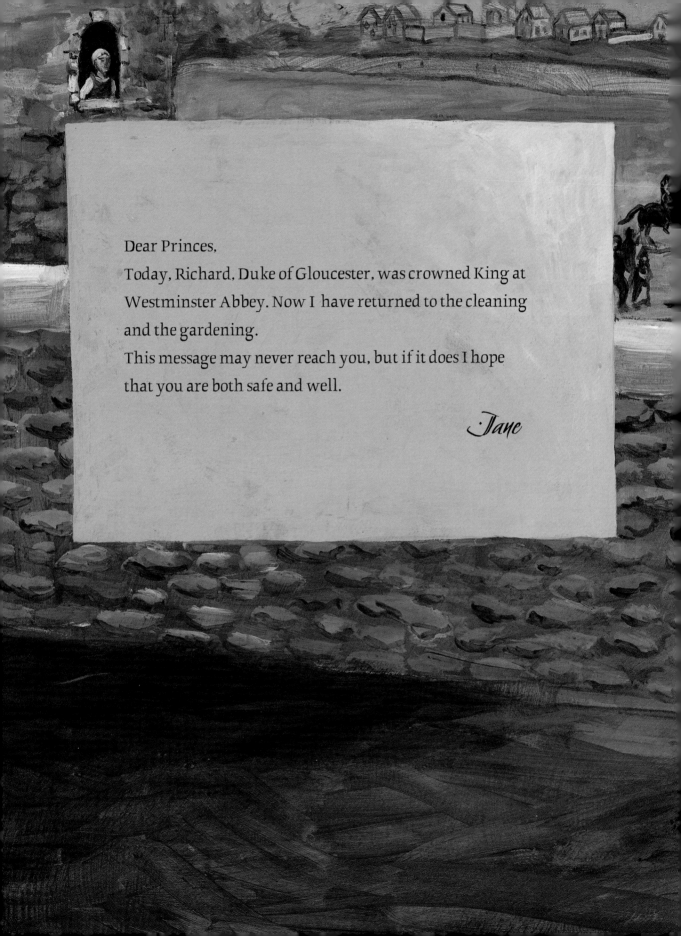

Dear Princes,

Today, Richard, Duke of Gloucester, was crowned King at
Westminster Abbey. Now I have returned to the cleaning
and the gardening.

This message may never reach you, but if it does I hope
that you are both safe and well.

Jane

Dear Jane,

We rowed through fog and were helped aboard a ship smelling of sweet spices. After an eternity, we reached a shore where it is very warm and green—and it is not damp! Thank you (and Jewel) for saving our lives. We will never forget you.

Always and still,

His Royal Highness Prince Edward

His Royal Highness Prince Richard

author's note

One of the great mysteries in the history of the English monarchy is the fate of Prince Edward and his younger brother, Prince Richard, known as "The Princes in the Tower." In 1483, their father, King Edward IV, died, leaving his eldest son to be crowned the next King of England. Their uncle, Richard, Duke of Gloucester, took the princes under his protection and placed them in the Tower of London. That summer, the princes vanished, and Richard, Duke of Gloucester, was crowned King Richard III.

Many believe that the duke had the princes killed, placing himself next in line for the crown. To this day, the true fate of the princes remains unknown. When one visits the Tower today, it is often explained simply that the princes were "lost from view."

There were many people, young and old, living and working at the Tower then, as now. Also in residence at the Tower are ravens, which have lived there for hundreds of years. They are the legendary protectors of the monarchy. It is believed that if the ravens ever leave the Tower, the monarchy will fall.

Chronology

1077 White Tower, first tower of the Tower of London,
built by William the Conqueror

1442 Birth of Edward IV, son of Richard, Duke of York

1452 Birth of Richard, Duke of Gloucester, brother of Edward IV

1455 Beginning of the "Wars of the Roses" between two branches
of the royal Plantagenet family—the House of York (White Rose)
and the House of Lancaster (Red Rose)

1461 Edward IV of the House of York claims the throne from
Henry VI of the House of Lancaster

1464 Marriage of King Edward IV to Elizabeth Wydville

1470 Birth of Prince Edward, first son and heir to Edward IV

1473 Birth of Prince Richard, second son of Edward IV

1483 Death of King Edward IV

Prince Edward and Prince Richard confined to the Tower of London
by their uncle, Richard, Duke of Gloucester

Princes last seen

Coronation of Richard, Duke of Gloucester, as King Richard III

1485 Henry Tudor, Earl of Richmond of the House of Lancaster,
challenges and defeats Richard III in the last of the Wars of the Roses

Death of Richard III

Coronation of Henry, Earl of Richmond, as Henry VII